Mail Order
The Bride Excnange

By
Faith Johnson

Clean and Wholesome Western
Historical Romance

Printed in the United States of America

Table of Contents

Unsolicited Testimonials

By **Glaidene Ramsey**
★★★★★ I so enjoy reading Faith Johnson's stories. This Bride and groom met as she arrived in town. They were married and then the story begins.!!!! Enjoy

By **Voracious Reader**
★★★★★ "Great story of love and of faith. The hardships we may have to go through and how with faith, and God's help we can get through them" -

By **Glaidene's reads**
★★★★★ "Faith Johnson is a five star writer. I have read a majority of her books. I enjoyed the story and hope you will too!!!!!"

By **Kirk Statler**
★★★★★ I liked the book. A different twist because she wasn't in contract with anyone when she went. She went. God provided for her needs. God blessed her above and beyond.

By **Amazon Customer**
★★★★★ Great clean and easy reading, a lot of fun for you to know ignores words this is crazy so I'll not reviewing again. Let me tell it and go

By **Kindle Customer**
★★★★★ Wonderful story. You have such a way of showing people that opposite do attack. Both in words and action. I am glad that I found your books.

FREE GIFT

Just to say thanks for checking our works we like to gift you

Our Exclusive Never Before Released Books

100% FREE!

Please GO TO

http://cleanromancepublishing.com/gift

And get your FREE gift

Thanks for being such a wonderful client.

Chapter One

Betty Marks returned the book to the shelf when Mrs. Kolb drifted off to sleep. It was her routine to do so after lunch and a cup of tea. Betty was the live-in companion to Mrs. Patience Kolb, the widow of Jeffrey Kolb, who died twenty years earlier. Having grown up in an orphanage, Betty was finally lucky when Mrs. Kolb chose her above a handful of other women competing for the job.

Betty would find out that she was selected because of her history of being an orphan—because Mrs. Kolb was one too. She had ended up married to a wealthy man and living in a mansion, and she wanted to share it with someone who would appreciate it. She also said the twenty-one-year-old Betty had a twinkle in her eye that none of the other girls possessed.

Betty loved the quiet moments in the library after Mrs. Kolb drifted off to sleep. The polished mahogany shelves were filled with treasures in the volumes they held. Betty had never imagined she'd have access to something so grand. She was reading *Robinson Crusoe* to Mrs. Kolb, and they both enjoyed hearing about his adventures. They both knew such adventures never happened in Dover, Delaware, which made it all the more fun to read.

Mrs. Kolb often said Betty was young enough to still experience adventure, but at eighty-two, her next adventure would be heaven.

"Betty, you're are so kind to linger after I fall asleep. It's my fear that I will die in my sleep with no one near me, and I will never be found to be buried next to my Jeffrey," she said. "I so cherish your company, but I dreamed you left me and embarked on a great adventure."

Betty *tssked.* "I'm never going to leave you, and I'll make sure you're buried next to Jeffrey where you belong. The opportunity you have given me will not be repaid by deserting you in your time of need. You need a companion, and I'm happy to be just that."

Mrs. Kolb had a halo of fluffy white hair and deep wrinkles that dominated her face. She was smaller every day, like she was slowly disappearing. Despite everything on the outside, her spirits were bright, and her mind was as sharp as a tack. Betty had come to think of her like a mother, and there were times she forgot Mrs. Kolb was simply the woman she worked for.

"Oh, Betty. I want for you what I had with my dearly departed Jeffrey. He changed my life and loved me in a way I didn't know possible. I never had to pretend to be anything except me. My heart soared when he entered the room, and when he was near, the smile on my face was never far."

"I'm happy with books, and I love the conversations we share," Betty said.

"My happiness comes from the wonderful memories I made and the adventures I lived. Now, mind you, they were nothing like the ones had by Robinson Crusoe. I worry about you at my age, with nothing to look back on," Mrs. Kolb said. "You mustn't forget the reality that soon I won't be here."

"Why are you being so insistent? Do you have a plan for me, Mrs. Kolb?" Betty asked.

"As a matter of fact, yes, I do. I have a friend who's a marriage broker, which is a fancy way of saying she arranges mail-order-bride situations for young women. Almost always, they are matched with a man in the west. She normally charges a fee, but of course, she would do it for you as a courtesy."

"I've heard girls who have traveled west, but I never imagined that life for me. With your friend, it sounds so easy. I guess I'll consider it more carefully, but only because you ask."

***

Betty watched as Mrs. Kolb got smaller and smaller, the train pulling away. Her goodbye was tearful, because she was never going to see the kind and intelligent woman again. Betty was going all the way to Denver to marry a barrister, Mr. Bill Chancellor. Girls like her were normally paired with a farmer or miner sort, but Mrs. Kolb thought Betty deserved better. She had gotten used to living in the big house, and there was no reason she should have to accept a less comfortable life. Betty didn't care so much, but Mrs. Kolb insisted, and so it was.

She sighed. She never would have left at all, but Mrs. Kolb had already decided to move in with her sister, Agnes. Agnes was recently widowed but had a larger house and servants she wanted to share with Patience. The sisters had always been close, and it seemed like a good change for everyone.

Betty walked through the train and looked for an open seat next to a woman so she would feel comfortable on the long journey. "Excuse me, would you mind me taking the seat next to you?" she asked the woman with a severe bun, who looked just as frightened as she felt.

"Of course. Please do. I was worried an unpleasant character might take that seat next to me, and I was told the journey could be lengthy. I'm Nan Brightenbush."

"I'm Betty Marks. You don't look familiar, but I've heard your name before. If you don't mind sharing, where did you grow up?" Betty asked.

"I'm not ashamed to say that I grew up at St. Agatha's Orphanage. It wasn't a perfect childhood, but what counts is how I handle the rest of my life. A kind nun at the orphanage told me that, and I think she's right," Nan said cheerfully.

"Was it Sister Christopher?" Betty asked.

"Yes!" Nan exclaimed. "You must know St. Agatha's."

"I do, because I grew up there too. Sister Christopher said something similar to me. I'm going as far as Denver to become a mail-order bride. What are you doing on the train?" Betty asked.

"The same thing. I've been arranged to marry Jason Dudley, a worker in a silver mine. He's smart and funny, and we've been exchanging letters for a year. He's hard-working and wants children, as do I. I want them to be loved by the people who brought them into the world because I know what it's like not to have that," Nan explained.

"I only know a small amount about my intended, as I went through a marriage broker who handled everything. His name is Bill Chancellor, and he's a barrister. Apparently, he's quite comfortable, and he's never been married." Betty paused. "I'm nervous. Are you? Or am I worrying about nothing?"

"I wasn't going to say anything, but I've been worrying day and night since Jason officially invited me to Denver. It's so bad that I can't sleep," Nan said.

"You're braver than I am, Nan, because I couldn't marry a miner. I've heard the job is dangerous, and there's a frequent chance that he won't make it home for dinner," Betty said.

"I thought about that, but Jason assures me the Denver mine is safe. He said they dig into solid bedrock and they've never had a cave-in. So I suppose I will just have to take his word for it.

"I didn't mean to cause you more worry. I can be such a ninny at times," Betty said, her cheeks flushing. "Saying whatever pops into my mind is a habit."

"I'm the same way." Nan laughed and, relieved, so did Betty.

Betty and Nan continued to find things they had in common, and it made travel go by quickly. Everyone around them complained about the mechanical difficulties in Chicago, which eventually caused them to switch trains. Nan and Betty thought it allowed them more time together, however, and their spirits were never dimmed.

Growing up without a sister made having one a dream of nearly every girl at the orphanage. Nan and Betty were certain that dream was finally coming true.

Chapter Two

Bill Chancellor was working in his study when there was a knock at the door. He hoped his mail-order bride hadn't arrived early, because he wasn't quite ready for her. He had work to finish before Betty's arrival so he would have plenty of time to get her settled. He pulled open the door.

"Francesca. What are you doing here?" Bill asked.

Francesca was the woman he had intended to marry—before she'd jilted him. She had departed Denver three weeks ago without so much as a goodbyc and had only left him a brief note. Francesca had said she was planning to marry another, and there was no further explanation.

"I just got back on the train. Will you still have me?" a teary Francesca asked. "My father made me write that note and tried forcing me to marry another. I couldn't, and finally, my father relented. I think my mother made him. Oh, Bill, I'm so sorry."

Bill took her into his arms. He was thrilled to have the woman he loved back, but he didn't know what to do with Betty Marks. Until Francesca's return, he'd had every intention of marrying his mail-order bride. He'd decided to marry immediately before he was foolish enough to risk love again. A business arrangement might be safer.

After a heartfelt reunion and a recommitment to becoming man and wife, Bill told Francesca about Betty. She felt horrible for interfering and said she would help make things right.

"You have to find a replacement. A man you know to be a good and honest man. If you choose right, she may even fall in love with him. I pray that she will."

"I can't think of anyone through my work as a barrister…at least not anyone who is good and honest," Bill said.

"You grew up nearby in Bright Valley. Is there anyone there that you can think of?" Francesca asked.

Bill thought for a moment before his eyes grew wide and a smile appeared on his face. "Cole Bleeker. He's the one, and if you lived in Bright Valley, you'd know him by his reputation as a generous person. He may not have a lot, but he gladly shares what he does have."

"If he's like that, you will have to offer him a sum to do this for you. After all, you will know the money will be well spent. Perhaps he'll buy something to make his new wife happy. Then I won't feel so guilty," Francesca said.

"I'll go to Bright Valley in the morning. Will you accompany me?"

"Yes. I can't imagine you being out of my sight for the slightest moment," Francesca cooed.

***

Cole Bleeker was inside his small house, located in the shadows of foothills. It had a roof and four walls, so it was plenty for him, as he lived alone. He was shy and had given up hope on marrying. Unfortunately, any women he had tried to know mistook his shyness for anger or disinterest.

His close friend, Jason, was getting a mail-order bride who was due to arrive in Denver soon. Cole had considered a mail-order bride himself, but with his shyness and lack of experience talking to women, he'd finally decided against it.

The smells of summer wafted through his one window. A vine of yellow honey flowers climbed up to the roof and started down the other side. He imagined that one day his house would be covered in the delicate white-and-yellow flowers. Cole supposed that wouldn't be such a bad thing.

A knock made him turn. Someone was at his door, which was odd since Cole rarely received visitors. He pulled open the squeaky door.

"Bill, I haven't seen you in years. Is there a problem at the mine?" Cole asked. Cave-ins were rare in the Bright Valley, but no one doubted that it would eventually happen.

"No, but my fiancée and I have a favor to ask you. One that I'll pay you handsomely for."

"Come in." Cole dusted off his one chair and offered it to the woman. He thought she was very kind, not to mention the less-than-perfect condition of his house.

“Unless I’m missing something, you haven’t taken a wife. Is my assumption correct?” Bill asked.

“Does it look like a woman lives here with me?” Cole said with a smile and chuckle.

Bill told his story, and Francesca added her own thoughts when necessary. Cole’s jaw dropped when the favor was officially asked. Bill went on to share what he knew about Betty Marks, which wasn’t much.

“What’s Betty going to say when she finds out she’s not marrying a barrister in a big house in Denver?” he asked. “I don’t think she’ll like it much that I’m a miner living in a small house.”

“What you lack in material things, you make up for in other ways. I wouldn't be asking you if I thought differently," Bill said. “Francesca insisted I ask someone whom I respect, and that’s what brought me here.”

Bill placed a thick envelope on the table. “Inside is one hundred and fifty US dollars. It’s yours to do with what you want. It’s your choice whether or not you ever tell Betty about it.”

Cole pushed the envelope back in Bill’s direction. “If I agree to take Betty as my wife, and I’m leaning in that direction, I won’t take your money for it. As you know, my needs are simple.”

“That might change when you have a wife and someday a family. So you hold on to it for one year, and if you can’t find a use for it, I’ll take it back,” Bill proposed.

The whole time Bill and Cole were chatting about the money and other details, Francesca was tidying up and throwing as much trash as she could find in the bin. She wanted Betty to feel as welcome as possible, as the experience of moving to Denver would be a lot on its own. When Betty found out Bill had been replaced with Cole, she'd be overwhelmed.

Francesca's dreams had come true when Bill accepted her back, and she wanted Betty to be happy too.

Cole stood straight, took off his hat, and offered Bill his hand. "You have a deal. Yesterday, I was planning for life as a bachelor, and now I'm preparing to meet the woman who will be my wife. Do you know if Betty plans on a large family?"

"She mentioned that she wants as many youngins' as the lord provides," Bill responded.

"I like the sound of that answer," Cole said.

I'll meet you at the train station tomorrow, and we'll meet Betty's train together," Bill said as he and Francesca linked arms.

Cole walked his guest to the door, which was only three steps away from his small house.

After they left, he began to think of practical matters, like where Betty was going to sleep and what she was used to eating. He was happy it was summer because it was the most beautiful time of year in Colorado. The flowers and sage blended to produce a fresh, sweet scent.

Cole didn't have much experience with women, but there was one woman who he remembered well—his mother. She'd taught him all about the flowers and trees in the area. Irene Bleeker had told him it was knowledge he could share with his wife someday.

Cole hoped those things interested Betty, because he didn't have much else.

Chapter Three

Denver was the next stop, so Nan and Betty adjusted their hair beneath their bonnets and tried in vain to smooth out the wrinkles on their dresses. Betty organized her bag and hoped her two trunks were still on board. When they changed trains in Chicago, she worried that they'd forgotten to transfer hers.

The two women—who had chatted for a week while on their journey—grew silent out of nerves. Finally, the train lurched and came to a stop. Both women sighed and smiled at one another. No matter what happened in Colorado, a strong friendship had been formed. It was their hope that Bill and Jason liked one another too.

Jason had told Nan he would carry a purple stalk of phlox he would pick from the meadow on his way to greet her. Sure enough, he was there waiting for Nan with a broad smile on his face. He was with two other men, who followed Jason as he hurried to meet her.

"Since I see Jason first, come along with me," Nan said as she dragged Betty by her hand. "His smile tells me all I need to know. It shows he's as happy to see me as I am him."

Betty watched as Jason offered Nan offered a hand with a large smile. It was clear they wanted to embrace but would wait until they were alone. They introduced themselves, but they looked like a couple who were reuniting after several years and had missed one another immensely.

"Jason, this is my dear friend, Betty Marks, from Delaware. We didn't know each other before getting on the train but found we had so much in common. For example, we've come to the same spot as mail order brides. Betty is meeting Bill Chancellor here. If you know who he is, please tell her, because she'll never find him in this crowd."

"Betty, I'm Bill Chancellor," he said. Bill was tall and distinguished, in a pinstriped vest. Next to him was an ordinary-looking man wearing a clean blue shirt and brown trousers.

"Bill, you're just as I imagined. Mrs. Morgenstern at the agency described you perfectly."

Bill smiled cordially and asked if he could have a private moment with the green-eyed brunette. He asked the friend who had been standing with him to see about her trunks. The other man smiled and nodded. He started for the train and looked back with a question.

“How will I know which trunks are yours?”

"Oh, of course, you need that information. They're blue and have my name on a tag: Betty Marks.”

“Thank you, Betty,” he said cordially.

Betty followed Bill to a spot under a tree where they benefitted from the shade.

“I appreciate the private moment. It was overwhelming with your friend and Jason next to us; this way, we can take time to properly introduce ourselves," Betty said.

A sympathetic smile grew on Bill's face. "I will not be marrying you today, and since you didn't know me, I took the step to find someone else for you to marry. I wasn't about to send you back to Delaware after you traveled so far. You will thank me for this someday, because Cole is a man with morals and intelligence. I have known him since we were both hiding in our mama's skirts."

"I don't understand. Did you see me and decide that I was not fit to be your wife?" Betty asked. She found she was not terribly bothered. Instead, in a way, she was satisfied she was not marrying a man who would go back on a promise he had made.

"The man who stood next to me and is fetching your trunks is Cole Bleeker. He'll marry you today, if the situation is acceptable to you. He has a house in a town not far from here. Bright Valley is where most of the mine workers live. Let me tell you why I'm unable to take you as my wife…"

Betty interrupted. "I don't want an explanation. At the moment, I don't think very highly of you, but rest assured, if I see you at church or anywhere else, I will nod and smile. I'm a lady, and I'll be going to meet Cole, the man I am going to marry." She walked away. Nan had mentioned Bright Valley as the place she would be living, and that made things better.

Cole was standing with Jason and Nan. Betty refused to think of the Bill situation as a setback. As she walked back towards the train area, she took a deep breath and loved what she smelled. Betty thought she'd miss the smells of the ocean, but she was wrong. There was a sweet sage scent in the air. When she looked up, Betty saw towering mountains with snow-covered tops. It was very warm, but not too hot, so it was funny that she could see the snow. She was determined to enjoy her Colorado life, despite not marrying Bill Chancellor.

Betty was determined to continue on with her head held high.

Cole had retrieved her trunks and already loaded them onto his wagon. The next stop was Bright Valley. First, however, she and Nan would officially become brides. They were headed for the courthouse in

Denver because Bright Valley was too small to have one of its own.

"Was this marriage idea surprising to you, Cole?" Betty asked after he had helped her up on the wagon.

"I was surprised, but I'm learning that surprises can be a good thing. I was beginning to think a wife and children weren't going to happen for me. I didn't have the courage to ask a woman to move here as Jason did. But it happened anyway, and I guess it was meant to be," Cole said.

"I guess that's the courthouse. Nan and Jason can't get up the steps fast enough. They shared letters for almost a year, and we hardly know a thing about each other. I suppose that means we'll have plenty to talk about." Betty was going to stay positive. That way of thinking had carried her through all the dark days at the orphanage.

Betty waited with Nan while Jason and Cole paid the necessary fees and filled out paperwork.

"Jason told me what he knows of the situation," Nan said. "It's not what you expected. I'm surprised you're willing to marry Cole, although I'm thrilled you are. He's a miner, and you mentioned how much being married to a man who risked his life daily would be horrible. Although, Jason says Cole is a loyal friend and the hardest worker he knows."

"I don't see that I have a choice but to marry Cole. It means we'll be close, and if Bill doesn't want to be my husband and Cole does, then it seems I'm doing the right thing.

How bad could it be? From what I see so far, Colorado is beautiful."

"I think so too. They're coming this way now. Remember, if you need anything, I'll be there," Nan said.

Betty squeezed her hand. "Thank you. I'll be there for you too."

Cole and Betty Bleeker went back to the wagon in silence, walking side by side. Nan and Jason Dudley walked out before them with hands held tight as they chatted.

Betty was a married woman, and now it was up to her to create a beautiful life with Cole.

Chapter Four

"We aren't terribly far from Bright Valley, but it gives us time to get to know each other beyond just our names," Cole said. "You can go first or me. Since you're the lady, you choose."

"You go, as my life might put you to sleep while you're guiding the team. Who knows where we'd end up." Betty chuckled. "I don't think ending up at the bottom of a ravine is a good way to begin my life in Colorado."

Cole cleared his throat. He noticed her uplifting and easily shared giggle, which put him at ease. "I was born right here in Bright Valley twenty-eight years ago. My father worked for the Bright Valley mine when they thought there'd be gold in the hills. He didn't die of a mine collapse, like so many others, but illness. He passed when I was about ten, so it's my mama who took care of me. I started at the mine young because I had to take care of her and put food on the table. That's been my life ever since."

Betty's hands curled into fists when he mentioned mining. She heard Bill say it, but hearing it from her husband made her worry. Betty had only just met Cole, but she sure wasn't prepared to see her husband die in the mine. "Is mining something you enjoy?"

"I do enjoy the men I work with. They're my family, and there isn't a thing I wouldn't do for any one of them. The best part is that they'd also do anything for me. It can be lonely out here, and they offer comfort."

"You aren't alone anymore. One thing you should know about me is that I adapt easily to any situation. I went from living in an orphanage where I slept in a room with ten other girls to living in a mansion," Betty said.

"How'd that happen? Were you adopted by a wealthy family?" Cole asked as they pulled closer to his home.

"No. I was hired as a companion to the widow of the former mayor of Dover. Why are we stopping here?"

"This is where we live," Cole said. "I know it's a far cry from the mansion you were used to. With a wife, I'll be forced to make it a more comfortable place to live."

Betty clenched her teeth and tried to think positively. It was more of a shack than a home, but it was her shack as Mrs. Bleeker, and improvements could be made. "As long as there's a hearth to keep us warm in the winter, it will be enough for now," Betty said with as much cheer as she could muster.

One room was split from the sleeping area by a sheet. Betty imagined Cole having just put it up when he found out she was coming. She appreciated small gestures like that because it showed he cared and wished some things were different. A fine layer of dust covered some surfaces and some had recently been wiped clean. There was only one chair and the table stood at a slant.

Betty scanned the room and wanted to run away, but that wasn't a choice. She had to find something to compliment… and she struggled to find a single thing.

“What do you think?” Cole asked. Betty noted that he sounded both hopeful and embarrassed.

"I can hardly focus due to the lovely scent coming through the window. There is a flower growing nearby I’ve never smelled before. It will be lovely to smell at night as I go to sleep.”

Cole seemed flattered that Betty had found something nice to say. “Your favorite thing about this place is mine too. I was just thinking about it today, and it seems to be more robust every summer. I call it a honey flower because that’s what it smells like to me.”

"I'll have to cut some and place it on the table so we can bring the lovely aroma into the house," Betty noted.

"Great idea. I must have a can or bottle around here somewhere." Cole said.

Betty went to the cupboards that lined a wall in the kitchen area. She opened the first cupboard and quickly slammed the door. "Nothing in there but a big rat. It's not the first rodent I've seen, but I am concerned that you don't seem to have any food supplies. Is there a root cellar?"

"I'm afraid not. I have a small barn with a larder and a cow I milk daily, although some days I'm too tired. The cow doesn't like that much. So there is a way to get milk and butter. There are half a dozen chickens in there, too, and I should be collecting eggs every day."

"I know what I'll be doing while you're in the mine. I'll try to get the barn organized and cleaned out. The animals will be more productive if they're happy. Where do you keep the flour and sugar, so I can at least bake some bread?"

"Um, I'm short on those things. There are a few jars of vegetables in the larder and some preserved meat. My friend Ben's wife, Diane, helps with canning when she's able. We have a garden, but the growing season in Colorado is short. I didn't get my seeds in early enough. I discovered that getting them in late doesn't give them enough time before the first frost arrives."

“To think I was worried about not having enough to do. Mrs. Kolb gave me some pin money before I left. All you have to do is point me to the nearest general store,” Betty chirped. “I’ll get the supplies necessary.”

“Don’t think of spending your own money. I’m your husband, and I’ll take care of all your needs.” Cole said emphatically.

Cole and Betty went into the barn and uncovered several crates he had from his mother. Just after she died of an illness that took her quickly, the house they were living in burned to the ground. These things were saved from the only room that wasn’t destroyed—the kitchen. Cole didn't know how to boil water for tea, so he’d never found a use for the things.

Betty was finding small flickers of light in a gloomy situation. There were bowls, pots, pans, and a few recipes she had taken the time to write.

"Cole, look at this. Is it written in your mother's hand?" Betty asked. "They all have the name Irene written in the corner."

Cole perked up when he heard the name Irene. Betty handed him one of the recipes. "This is my mother's beautiful cursive. She learned it from the Catholic nuns. Her handwriting was as beautiful as she was and brings back a memory I had forgotten. I wouldn't have come upon this if not for you. Thank you."

Betty smiled but still felt a bit uneasy. She was living in a shack with a miner, and not in a mansion married to Bill Chancellor.

Cole couldn't be any nicer, but Betty was having a hard time adjusting to her new situation, despite some sweet moments.

Chapter Five

Betty pulled the dilapidated wagon under a maple tree so the horses could enjoy the shade. A trough of water was available, as the summer sun made the animals extra thirsty. She had sent Cole off to work in the mine after a breakfast of porridge. He'd assured her that Diane was in the habit of packing him a lunch pail because Cole and Ben walked together daily to the mine.

Betty couldn't decide if she was going to cook or clean, and the beautiful sunshine had made going into town for supplies an easy third choice.

A blue clapboard building with a wide front porch was her destination, along with a church and a saloon that made up most of the

Bright Valley town center. A creek was running beside the church, making a pleasant gurgling sound. The bell on the door chimed as she walked into Weatherly's General store. A woman with a round face and welcoming smile greeted Betty.

"Good morning. You're a new face, and I'm guessing you're Betty Bleeker," she said.

Betty was surprised. "Either I met you before and don't remember it, or you're good at guessing."

She giggled. "I saw Cole this morning when he came by to pick up Ben. I'm Diane, his wife, and I've been looking out for Cole. I prayed a nice woman would come along and marry him, not that I mind looking out for him. I just thought a man as kind and generous as Cole deserves someone to share his life with."

"How did you know it was me?" Betty inquired.

"Cole described you as having braided brown hair and green eyes that are so bright, they could be seen across the room. That and the fact that I've never seen you before," Diane explained. "My uncle owns the store, and his daughter usually stands behind the counter, but her third child came along last night. So I said I'd help out until she recovers because the birth was quite an ordeal."

"Every person I met since arriving in Colorado has been nice and welcoming. The moment I stepped off the train, all I saw were smiles. I look forward to everything this beautiful place has to offer," Betty said. "The mountains are awe-inspiring and provide a perfect backdrop to all the flowers."

"I heard what happened with Bill Chancellor. If you ask me, you got lucky when Francesca came back to claim his heart. He's nice and he has a lot of money, but his heart was always going to be with her. He grew up in Bright Valley, which is how I know him so well. Cole is big-hearted and willing to help anyone in need, even if it's not to his advantage. He could have had any woman he wanted if he had more confidence. But he's a little shy," Diane said.

Betty felt poorly inside because of the complaints she was making inside her head. She thought the house was too small and dirty and balked when there were no supplies. "It's nice to hear about Cole from someone who knows him well. It would be horrible to marry a mean-spirited man."

"Excuse me, Diane. Did I hear you mention Cole Bleeker?" an older woman asked. "I hate to intrude, but I hear he's gotten himself a wife. Is that true?" She asked.

"Mrs. Ansonia, I'd like you to meet Cole's wife. This is Betty Bleeker, so yes, it's true," Diane said.

"Oh, you are a lucky girl. I was only asking because my niece is coming to visit. I thought I'd introduce them if he were still single. She will have to look elsewhere for a husband, but how fortunate for you. I'm a widow and have no one to do things around the house. Cole has come to my aid on several occasions."

"I've only been married one day and have been in Colorado that same amount of time. From what I hear from everyone, I'm very fortunate to be Cole Bleeker's wife."

"Indeed. The two of you are welcome to come to visit at any time. Cole knows where I live. Ta, ta ladies." Mrs. Ansonia floated away in her billowy black dress.

When she was out of earshot, Diana told Betty all about the Widow Ansonia. Her husband was the manager at the mine. Although she had money to move anywhere she wanted, she stayed in Bright Valley after her husband's death. He was hit by a falling boulder in the mine, and she wanted to stay near the site where she could feel his spirit the strongest. Most thought she was eccentric, but Diane believed she added to the character of Bright Valley.

"I've so enjoyed chatting that I almost forgot the purpose of my visit." Betty handed her a list of her needs.

"It seems you need just about everything. The stock boy is here today, and I should know, as he's my son, Thomas. I'll have him load all of this onto your wagon. I assume it will go on Cole's account, is that right?" Diane asked.

"I have the money, so I'll pay this time. You said he's generous, so this once, I'll be generous towards him," Betty said.

Diane told Betty the areas could see the most beautiful flowers bloom. She also mentioned a small lake that attracted beautiful butterflies and delicate hummingbirds each summer. She told Betty it was not to be missed in the summer months.

"I'm so happy I came in today. You gave me a whole new perspective on life in Colorado and my husband, Cole. It's nice to hear he's so well thought of." Betty prepared to leave when Diane called her back.

"Betty, you've heard so much good about Cole, but never lose sight of your own accomplishments. Not everyone is brave enough to travel as far as you did and marry a complete stranger. Not to mention, upon arrival, you learned the man you were going to marry was no longer available. I would still be in tears from the shock of it all. You and Cole are both exceptional people, and that's why I'm sure you'll enjoy years of happiness," Diane said sincerely.

"Thank you, Diane. Cole and I would love to have you visit some afternoon. Do you know Jason Dudley?"

"We grew up together. I know him like a brother," Diane said.

"Is he a good man too?"

Diane smiled. "Good as gold."

Betty rode home and unpacked her supplies in the cupboards. She cleaned out barrels to hold the sacks of flour and oats, which she placed on wood frames to keep them off the ground. It's something she learned in the kitchen at St. Agatha's, to make it more difficult for rats to break in. It looked like the oven hadn't been used in years, so Betty spent hours cleaning off the rust and dirt using a chisel. A pile of chopped wood that was home to a little family of chipmunks provided what she needed to get the oven heating. Betty gathered nearby pine boughs and other fallen branches to try and give the chipmunks an alternative place to live, but they didn't seem interested.

Betty milked the cow, collected the eggs, and whistled as she worked. She cleared a rack for preserved meat high about the ground to keep away the varmints and covered everything with a flour sack. The smokehouse was located behind Jason's house. It was shared by several families, including the Bleekers. It was the responsibility of the men that enough meat was available to see them through winter. They did the hunting, trapping, and fishing.

She washed clothes and the filthy sheet in the brook that ran behind the barn. The summer air would have everything dry in a couple of hours.

Betty was exhausted but proud of the work she had accomplished. Finally, she fell asleep on the surprisingly comfortable bed and enjoyed the warm air and scent of the honey flower flowing through the window.

Chapter Six

Mr. Egan blew the whistle signaling the end of the shift in the mine. Cole was working on a team with Jason and Ben as he always was. Talking to good friends helped pass the time, and they all looked out for each other.

"Ready to head up and breathe some clean mountain air," Jason said.

"Just waiting for you to lead us out of here. I'm looking forward to a delicious dinner. Everything Diane makes is better than the last thing she made," Ben said. "What about you, Cole? Is the new wife up to preparing a meal yet? If she's not, Diane will share whatever she prepared for our family."

"I have faith Betty will have something waiting for me. All I really need is her when

I walk through the door. I’ve never looked forward to going home before, but now I do. I haven’t known her for but a day, but it was a good day, and I can’t wait for more,” Cole said.

“Good to hear. I thought I was the only one. Nan is all I wished for and more. She was talking about visiting on Sunday after church,” Jason mentioned.

“That sounds fine. Betty often talks about Nan and the bond they formed on their journey.”

“You’ve never been to church as far as I know,” Ben commented to Jason as they walked down to the stream to wash some of the soot from their faces.

"It's Nan's idea. She said she wants the church in our children's lives, so I’ll start now. It can't hurt. I used to go with my family when I was little," Jason replied.

The three of them began walking home together. Cole felt good about not being the only one who wasn't married. His house was first, and something felt different as he approached the door. It was a good feeling—he wasn't dreading another night alone.

The first thing he noticed was the clean smell of the air. Betty must have had the front door open all day. Then he saw a bunch of flowers in a jar on the table. He heard Betty's gentle breathing from behind the sheet, which was no longer covered in stains. Cole pulled back the fabric, and Betty stirred.

She sat up straight. "Cole," Betty said with a sleepy grin on her face. "Have you been home long? Am I dreaming?"

"No, not long at all, and you aren't dreaming. I almost walked out as soon as I walked in because I figured I was in the wrong place. It's clean, and I haven't seen it this way since the day I moved in. I get nervous sometimes, because my mother said cleanliness is next to Godliness, which means I'm in some serious trouble. You worked miracles, and the flowers on the table were very nice. Do I smell bread baking?" Cole asked.

"Yes. I'm your wife, and I'll be darned if Ben's wife, Diane, makes you lunch ever again." Betty giggled. "You can expect bread and butter every day, because I'll churn each morning. The cow was so happy to see me. I even gave her the name Mary, which I think she likes. When I say it, she swirls her tail."

"I'll bet. I allowed her to get swollen, and that can't feel good," Cole noted. "The cow isn't the only one happy to have you here. I don't know how I lasted this long without you."

Betty felt her face warm. She had worked hard, and the compliment made it worth it. If hard work put a smile on Cole's face, she'd continue doing it every day.

Cole helped Betty onto her feet, and they both smiled as their touch on one another's hand felt wonderful and natural.

"I hope you're hungry. I used your mother's recipe to make pea soup with ham. I'm serving it with biscuits as she recommends," Betty said.

Cole turned away. Betty was surprised as they seemed to be having an idyllic evening so far.

“Cole, did I say or do something to disturb you?” Betty asked as she tied an apron around her waist before serving.

“No, quite the opposite. I turned away because I was overcome with emotion. I’m not used to other people seeing me this way." Cole turned towards Betty as a single tear rolled down his cheek. “I haven’t had pea soup since Irene Bleeker was alive, and it brought up a memory I didn’t know I had.”

“I’m glad. So let's sit at the table and eat your mother's soup together. I can tell you some ideas I had about the house.”

"Sounds great. I hope you put the things from the general store on my account," Cole said.

"Umm, I used my money this one time," Betty said. "I know we have to watch our pennies since you don't make a lot of money."

"Betty, I have…" Cole started to say.

She interrupted. "I don't care what amount you have. What else was I going to spend money on?" Betty asked rhetorically.

Cole placed a spoonful of soup in his mouth, and his eyes grew to double their size. "I feel like I'm at the table, and my mother has just served me her soup. How did you get it to taste so heavenly?" he asked.

"She had a few herbs in her recipe with which I wasn't familiar. I worked in the kitchen at St. Agatha's, and we never used any herbs except a scant bit of salt. Mrs. Kolb liked a lot of different herbs, though, so I figured I'd see what is growing in the area. I know what rosemary looks like, so I searched for it in the field behind the house. I found it, and that's what the unique flavor is. It looks like pine needles but doesn't taste that way."

"You could prepare this soup every day, and I'd never tire of it," Cole said.

Betty shared her idea of adding another window to the small house and perhaps a front porch. Cole liked both ideas and could have the window finished by fall and maybe the porch too. Betty was thrilled that he was open to her suggestions, and he was glad she was planning for the long term. Before Betty arrived, he imagined she'd take one look at him and hop on the next train heading east.

"Is there anything else you can think of changing?" Cole asked.

"I wish you didn't risk your life in the mine every day," Betty said, knowing that wouldn't change.

Cole shook his head. "It's all I can do to make money in these parts. My father earned his living in the mine, so it was natural for me to do it too."

"My biggest fear is that you work beneath a pile of rocks that could collapse at any moment. You do it because your father did, so does that mean you expect our son to do the same?" Betty asked. She was curious how Cole would act when he heard the mention of a child, as that was something they hadn't spoken of.

Cole looked surprised in a happy way. “No, our child can be president of the United States if he wants to. He won’t know the limits I had. Bill told me you wanted a family, but you haven’t mentioned it. I thought you may have changed your mind after seeing my small house.”

“No. Part of the reason I came was that Bill wanted to have a big family. I would have been sad if you didn’t feel the same way.”

Things were working out better than Betty could have imagined. They were not as she had expected, but she believed God had a plan that threw her and Cole together. Bill showed that he went back on his word, and

Cole was the opposite. He would never keep anything important from her, and that was a quality she treasured.

Chapter Seven

Weeks passed, and Betty started to feel like she belonged in Bright Valley. She knew everyone who lived in the small town and most of the men worked in the mine. Betty learned it was natural to have worries about a mine collapse, and she also learned that there hadn't been one in thirty years. Five men perished then, and the rest were able to escape to safety. Still, every night Cole walked up the steps to their small home, she celebrated inside.

Cole sawed a hole in the back of the house where a window would be placed. Betty soon realized the house wasn't as small as it looked. They'd ordered the glass from Denver, and it would be ready any day. Betty chose gingham fabric from the store to make curtains and used ribbons to tie them back when necessary. The ribbons had been gifts from Mrs. Kohl when she left. Betty had intended to use them in her hair, but thought they would be put to better use in the house. She wanted to put them up before Nan came over for tea. They lived less than a mile from each other but seldom found the time to visit.

Colleen Weatherly was behind the counter at the store with a baby on her hip. "Hello, Colleen. I'm going to take three yards of the yellow gingham fabric," Betty said. "You can put it on the Bleeker account."

"Oh, I love the yellow. It's such a hopeful color, and I'm sure everyone in the mine has a lot of hope this unusually warm summer," she said.

Betty had no idea what Colleen was talking about. It was warm but not sweltering. “I’m new to the area, as you know, so I don’t know how the hot weather affects the mine. Please explain.”

She thought she wanted to be informed, but then considered maybe it wasn’t the best idea. Betty was already concerned there would be a mine collapse, despite Cole telling her it was safe.

Too late now, though. Colleen was about to tell her all about it.

“When it’s hot, the snow melt increases. Simply put, that loosens the soil below, and where the water gathers, it puts pressure on solid walls. They mostly deal with solid walls, which means they’re very thick and usually safe. But if the pressure builds up enough behind that wall, it could burst through," Colleen said.

"How the heck do you know that? You sound like a scientist," Betty said.

"My brother is a scientist. Instead of sticking around Bright Valley, he went back east to study. No one thought he was very smart, but he was curious about everything and left Colorado to find answers," Colleen explained.

Betty left the general store with her fabric and a lot of new knowledge. However, she had facts that would make her worry more than ever. She wondered whether or not she should say something to Cole, but she decided not to. He was a miner, and nothing she could say would change that.

Anyway, besides Betty's husband going to the silver mine six days a week, life in Colorado was wonderful.

***

The Dudleys joined Betty and Josh by the small lake Diane had described. The cove was tucked away, and the cool breeze coming off the water felt heavenly on a hot summer day. They had all gone to Sunday services, although Cole and Jason would have rather been resting on their only day off. Nan and Betty appreciated the effort. When children came along, their workloads would be more equal, although the women wouldn't have Sunday free.

"Diane was right when she told me it was a wonderful place to see butterflies and hummingbirds. The colors are amazing, and the creatures so delicate," Betty remarked.

"They're both attracted to the nectar of the flowers that grow here. So where one gathers, you can normally see the other. The red poppies are a favorite of the hummingbird. For some reason, the color attracts them," Cole said.

Betty was astounded by his knowledge. "How did you learn so much about the animals, insects, and flowers?"

Cole blushed. He didn't mean to attract attention to himself. There were times Betty forgot Cole was painfully shy. He had shed that part of his personality when he was alone with Betty.

"After my father died, it was just my mother and me. We spent all our time together, and she shared what she knew about the beauty of the outdoors. If her eyes were closed and a flower was placed under her nose, she could identify it. Irene Bleeker never gave a wrong answer. Over time, her knowledge wore off on me."

"You were lucky to have a mother. That's something Betty and I never knew, and I think that's why we'll make the best mothers," Nan said. "We should make it a point to come here more often after services on Sunday. When we have little nippers, they can play in the water, and I do hope that happens soon. Isn't that a good idea, Jason?" she asked as she nudged her husband, who had drifted off to sleep.

"What? Yes, no matter the question, I agree with you, Nan," a groggy Jason said jokingly.

Cole laughed. "You learned quickly to agree with your wife. It seems like a good idea with a clever woman like Nan. She's like Betty in that most of her ideas are better than those I can come up with."

Nan blushed. "Thank you for the compliment."

"I'd say we're both fortunate to have ended up with our lovely wives from Delaware," Jason said. "I've been meaning to ask you, Cole, did you figure out what to do with the money from Bill Chancellor?"

Betty's head snapped, and Nan was confused by the question.

"Bill Chancellor gave you money? What was it for?" Betty asked.

"Did you sell him silver you got from the mine? I didn't think you were supposed to do that," Nan said. "You could lose your job if such an indiscretion was uncovered."

Jason knew immediately he had said the wrong thing. "I think this is a matter for Cole and Betty to discuss privately. Let's head home. We'll walk together as always, right, Cole?"

"I'm not working until late tomorrow. I'm staying past dark to help Mr. Egan as he lays explosives for a new mine entrance. He said I can come in late in exchange for doing him the favor. So you and Ben will be shorthanded, but I think you'll be fine."

They rode off. Betty knew there was something Cole didn't want to talk about, so she had to insist. "Why did Bill Chancellor give you money?" she asked for a second time.

"It was nothing that you need to concern yourself with. It wasn't much, but he owed me a favor, and he paid me. Bill grew up in Bright Valley, so things with us go back a long way," Cole answered.

"I've believed everything you've ever said to me, but this is different. Jason left in a hurry, so he thought it was a big deal. Perspiration is gathering on your top lip, so I know you're nervous. Please tell me the truth," Betty pleaded.

"Let's go home and we can talk about it there."

Betty walked to the wagon. She feared Cole was stalling so he could come up with a believable answer. All she wanted was the truth so they could move on.

Chapter Eight

The ride home was silent as Cole navigated the wagon along the dry path. The heat had been something Betty hadn't been bothered by since she arrived in Colorado. However, after her conversation with Colleen and how the heat might affect the mine, it began to weigh heavy on her mind.

Betty heated the chicken stew she had made the night before. She was proud of the meal and expected positive comments from her husband, but he said nothing.

"Are you enjoying the stew?" Betty asked to break the silence.

Cole nodded and said nothing.

"I refuse to let the sun set before we resolve this issue. All I ask is that you tell me why Bill Chancellor gave you money. Only then can we begin working on the issue, because right now, we can't even speak to one another. I know that isn't good for our young marriage," Betty said.

Cole eventually raised his head and looked at Betty for the first time since their argument started. "This happened before I met or married you. It's part of my past and, therefore, my concern alone. Therefore, I ask you to leave this matter be."

"No. You're secretive regarding this matter, which makes me believe it's something you desperately want to keep me from knowing. If you aren't honest with me, I'll be forced to go to Bill Chancellor, and I have no reason to believe he won't tell me everything."

"It's not fair to bring him or his wife, Francesca, into this. But, if you must know, Bill paid me one hundred and fifty dollars to marry you when he could no longer fulfill the commitment," Cole admitted. "I had already made up my mind to take you as my wife, and I tried refusing the money, but he insisted."

"It doesn't seem that you tried very hard, as you accepted it," Betty said harshly. She wasn't as mad as much as she was pained and embarrassed.

"He proposed that I keep the money for one year. He said I might need it with a wife and someday children. I didn't see a choice but to accept, and when you needed cooking supplies, I tried giving you a portion, but you refused," Cole explained.

“Do you still have the money?” Betty asked.

“I spent some of it on glass for the new window and supplies for the porch,” Cole said.

“You should have told me, and I would have understood… not right away, but eventually,” she said.

“Are you telling me I’ll never be forgiven?” he asked.

“I’m not going to throw away what we’ve built and will hopefully continue to build. But I need time to think and make sure I’ll be able to trust you as I did before. So I’m going to spend time in the barn with the animals. I have chores to finish, and I need to work this matter out in my head.”

"I hate that I deceived you. Please don't let this issue linger. You have brought such joy to this house. I don't even notice how small it is anymore. I like it small, because it means I have to be nearer to you," Cole said tenderly.

It took everything in her not to run into his arms and forgive him, but she needed time.

Betty left Cole sitting at the table and went out to the barn. She let her defenses down only after she was alone and began to sob uncontrollably. Betty had spent years in the orphanage. As a result, she had difficulty trusting anyone. She was afraid she would be abandoned, as her mother had done to her as an infant. Finally, she had learned to trust again with the help of Mrs. Kolb, and Betty gained the confidence she needed to leave Delaware and begin a life of her own.

Now there were cracks in her resolve, and she was searching for the strength to forgive her husband.

Betty fell to her knees and prayed. She wished Mrs. Kolb was next to her so she could ask her how to pardon Cole and forget about the lie he had told. Just then, there was a knock on the barn door. Betty thought for sure it was Cole.

She swung open the door, and the night air rushed in. “Hello, I don’t think we’ve met, so let me introduce myself. I’m Francesca Chancellor, Bill’s wife. I’m sorry to come so late, but I heard you know of your husband's payment.”

"Come in. How did you know, and how did you know I was in the barn?" Betty asked.

"I waited in the carriage and saw you walk out here and not go back in the house. I found out because word travels. Bill grew up in this town, and his connections run deep. I've wanted to speak to you about this matter since you arrived in Denver."

"I don't think I would have spoken to you back then. My feelings were bruised when Bill said he was no longer going to marry me. I didn't know the details but only picked up pieces of it along the way. You and I are now married to the people we are meant to be with. Is there a more specific reason for your visit?" Betty asked.

"Yes, the money was my idea, if that matters in any way. I'm the reason Bill did not marry you, and I felt horrible that he had to break the commitment. I almost didn't come forward and ask because it didn't feel right to interfere with your plans. I told Bill he had to give Cole something. Cole did refuse the money, and I know that because I was in the house at the time," Francesca assured her.

"I can see this ordeal has pained you. I don't harbor animosity toward you. Love makes us do things we otherwise might not do. It's the lie that I'm having a hard time forgiving, and if you can help me with that, I'd be forever grateful."

Francesca agreed to help her work through her problem. She was happy, too, because Bill was away on business and she had nowhere to be. They spoke for hours, and

Betty learned to trust herself and her feelings. Until she did that, it was impossible to trust another person. Francesca told her that arguments are bound to happen, along with misunderstandings. Still, we can learn from them and make our marriages stronger.

They were laughing and telling stories for hours. Finally, Betty realized the sun had risen, and she decided to forget about the payment. It was more important to focus on the present than what happened in the past.

"Your poor carriage driver has been waiting all night," Betty said as they got up from the hay bales they used to sit on. I hope he was able to sleep or at least enjoy the stars."

They walked to the barn door. Betty was pleased Cole had gone to bed early. She could fix him breakfast, and they could spend time together before he had to be at the mine with Mr. Egan.

Betty stepped out to a giant plume of smoke in the sky. Her heart stopped when she thought of the mine, but she was relieved when she remembered Cole wasn't working until later in the day. She walked Francesca to her carriage and thanked her for coming. Neither knew exactly what to think of the smoke in the air.

Betty opened the door to the house and found Cole about to leave in his mining clothes. He rushed towards the door and walked out.

"I have to go to the mine. There has been an explosion," Cole said, and he was gone before Betty could say a word. She had no idea what was happening, only that she had to follow her husband.

Chapter Nine

Betty rode on horseback to the mine and didn't pass Cole on the way as she had hoped. He must have run like the wind. When she approached the mine entrance, there was a gathering of women, including Nan and Diane.

"Nan, tell me what happened," Betty said to her friend, whose face was red and tear-stained.

"There was an explosion. It may have been a flood at first, but then the mine collapsed. Some men made it out, but others are still inside. Those miners include Jason and Ben," Nan said tearfully.

"Cole ran out before I could say a word to him, and I'm sure he's around here somewhere," Betty noted. "We will wait and pray because that's all we can do now."

"I've been doing that, and it hasn't helped Jason or me. I'm carrying my first child and just told him about it before he left for work this morning. We were the happiest we've ever been, and now this."

"I'm here for you, Nan, and won't leave your side. I see Mr. Egan, and he's coming this way. He has probably seen Cole and knows where he is. He might also have information about the trapped miners."

Mr. Egan stopped in front of the two women. "It's a terrible tragedy, and we are doing everything we can to return your husband to safety. I tried to stop Cole, but he insisted he knew the area where Ben and Jason were last seen. I'll keep you updated. In the meantime, I would return to your homes and go about your day. Unfortunately, there's nothing more you can do here."

He seemed to be trying to get rid of the woman because he had no answers for them.

"Mr. Egan, I'm confused. Cole wasn't among those trapped in the mine. Where is he?" Betty asked. She was bewildered about the change of events.

"Cole went into the mine with a pickax before anyone could stop him. He said he was going to rescue his friends or die trying," Mr. Eagan said and then shook his head in dismay. "I'm sorry, Mrs. Bleeker. Cole was single-minded, and there was nothing anyone could have done to stop him."

Mr. Egan began walking away, but Betty grabbed his elbow. "You just used the past tense when referring to my husband. I expect you to act like every miner trapped inside that mountain is alive. You owe us at least that, and we won't be returning to our homes until they come walking out of there. Nothing is more important to any of us than bringing our men home."

"Yes, Mrs. Bleeker," Mr. Egan said. There was no further discussion after Betty spoke.

When he had gone, Diane turned to Betty. "They always said they would risk their lives for each other. So I'm not surprised Cole followed through on his word. It's the type of man we all know he is. I thank God my son Thomas wasn't around, or he would have joined your husband." As Diane spoke, she looked into the distance. A small caravan of wagons was heading their way, and no one had an explanation.

A carriage that looked familiar to Betty led the caravan. It was Francesca Chandler's that she had seen earlier in the day. Betty wondered what she was doing at the mine.

"I'm sure you ladies are surprised to see us, but we want to lend our support in any way we can. For starters, we brought food and water, so you don't have to go home, and you can be right here where your men need you. We also have a doctor and a couple of nurses who can help when the men come out," Francesca said. She was soon joined by her husband Bill, who got news of the cave-in while he was at the courthouse.

"I hope my presence doesn't bother you, Betty. I was born in Bright Valley, and my heart remains here. Francesca told me about your disagreement with Cole regarding my payment to him. I’m sorry for my part in it,” Bill said.

“The whole thing is so far from my mind. I just want my husband back so we can put it all behind us and continue with our happy marriage. Of course, I'm not bothered by your presence," Betty said with a light smile.

“I should let you know that all this help is funded by the Widow Ansonia, who was the one who organized everything. She has been in touch with the mine owner, and he knows of an entrance that hasn’t been used in years. So volunteers are looking into that now,” Bill explained.

Betty's heart was full as she looked around and saw how many people cared. She'd expected to feel completely alone while waiting, but the reality was much different. It didn't lessen her broken heart, but it helped her believe things would work out.

Nan and Diane took Betty's hand and led her to a circle of about twenty people who were praying to God. She joined, and they prayed for the survival of her loved ones.

***

Cole walked through the rubble along the narrow path that he, Ben, and Jason took six days a week. He never had a brother, but the bond he shared with them was as strong as if they were family. With each step he took, Cole thought of them, of course, but he also thought of Betty. His life started when she walked into it. All he wanted to do was walk out with his men and into the arms of his wife. She wasn't worth $150; no price could be paid for what she meant to him.

Cole arrived at the end of the path, and a wall of rocks stood in his way. His friends were trapped behind that wall and would soon run out of air. The wall was made up of thousands of head-sized boulders. Cole heard voices, but they were coming from behind him, not behind the wall as he had hoped.

"My guess is that you're Cole," a man said.

"Good guess. Who the heck are you?"

“We're volunteers, some of us with experience and some who just want to help. There's a woman out there who wants you to come out alive. I promised I would do everything to make that happen."

“I’m pretty sure they’re behind this mess of rocks, but there’s no way I can get through this. Did the woman have the most brilliant green eyes you’ve ever seen?” Cole asked.

"That was her. I'm Fred, and I worked in a mine before and ran up against something like this. We have a lot of help, so we can get through, but first, we have to make sure they're alive back there. Use this tin cup and bang against the rocks. If they bang back, we get to work.”

Cole banged the cup and called at the top of his lungs but received no response. The others told him it was hopeless, but then he heard a faint tapping. Cole banged again, and they tapped back. They began to dismantle the wall of rocks.

***

The sun was setting and spirits were getting low. Not one of the women had been reunited with their loved ones.

"What are we going to do, Betty? I can't survive as a young widow with a child, and I have nowhere else to go. I loved Jason before I came here, and that has increased tenfold. I never believed that there was one person on this earth for me, but now I do, and that one person was Jason." Nan caught another tear before it ran down her face.

"That person *is* Jason, not *was*. We must keep the faith because if the roles were reversed, we'd want them to hold out hope. When Jason walks out of that mine, he'll want to see a smile on your face and not tears."

Betty wasn't sure where she was getting her strength to be a comforter to so many who seemed to be losing hope. She never thought of herself as special, but then she remembered what Diane had said to her weeks ago. She reminded Betty that she was uniquely brave, and perhaps she was realizing that was true.

Betty had her eyes on the opening when she saw movement. At first, she thought her eyes were playing tricks on her, but then she heard a voice calling her name…it was Cole!

Chapter Ten

The sun had fallen behind the mountain, so it was hard to make out his face at first, but the voice was his.

"Come. They're coming out," Betty called to the others.

Cole carried a weak but alive Jason in his arms. He faintly said his wife, Nan's, name. Cole laid him down and ran to Betty. She fell into his grimy arms, and he repeated one phrase repeatedly. "I love you. I love you. I love you. I feared I would never see you again to tell you how much I love you. Not a day in my life will go by without telling you how much I love you."

"I'm sorry for the misunderstanding. I came in to tell you that I overreacted, but there was no stopping you. I love you too, and from now on, we'll not spend one night away from one another. I want you to wake up by your side always." Betty stopped talking only when Cole kissed her.

Only one man perished in the mine accident, which was considered a miracle. Diane and her boys took Ben home, who had injured his leg. Jason had cuts and bruises that would heal with time, and Nan was happy to tend to his wounds. But, before they left the mine site, Mr. Egan had something to say.

"Everyone acted with bravery today. The mine is a little damaged, but as a team, we can dig through the rubble and start mining silver once again. I received a telegram from Mr. Tanner, who owns the mine, and he has a surprise for each and every one of you…

Betty squeezed Cole's arm. "I hope it's a week off with pay. Goodness knows you all deserve it. Of course, I'd rather you never come back here."

Cole whispered back. "We would have to become suddenly rich for that to happen, but that's a dream I don't see coming true. It doesn't matter, though, because I have you."

Mr. Egan continued. "You do not have to report to work tomorrow, and you will get five dollars pay for not showing up."

The walking wounded and their wives clapped half-heartedly. They had nearly died and were supposed to be excited about coming back.

Betty and Cole laced arms and rode back together. Nothing could dim their relief and gratitude, not for anything. They walked into their charming home, which was the new word they used to describe it. It was no longer a small house and never again called a shack.

They sat in chairs behind the house and looked up at the sky dense with stars. “When you see a shooting star, you’re supposed to make a wish,” Betty said.

“My mother told me that you were never to utter the wish out loud, or it wouldn’t come true,” Cole noted.

“Oh, fooey, then don’t wish on a star. Just tell me what you would want if you could have one dream come true. I’ll go after you,” Betty chirped.

“I hated today because my friends were in harm's way, and I should have been with them. If it hadn’t turned out well today, I would have felt guilty forever. That wasn’t the worst part, though. It was the pain I caused you, and it’s something I will continue to do every day when I go work. If I had one wish, it would be not having to go to the mine and make you worry,” Cole said. “Now it’s your turn.”

“If I had one wish, it would be you finding something to do that you love. You know so much about trees and different types of wood. You could be a carpenter and never have to set foot in the mine again,” Betty said, then sighed. “Dreaming is fun as long as you’re not too disappointed when dreams don’t come true.”

“My biggest dream comes true every morning when I open my eyes and see you,” Cole said before leaning over and kissing his wife.

They had never slept so peacefully, as they were both exhausted after an eventful day. They planned to spend the day with the butterflies and hummingbirds. Cole was going to tell Betty about as many flowers as he could identify. It was going to be a blissful day in the Bleeker house.

Betty was fixing coffee when there was a knock at the door. Cole answered it as he always did when he was home.

“Hello, I am here to speak with Mrs. Betty Bleeker.”

Betty stepped forward. He spoke immediately and in a monotone. "I am representing the estate of Mrs. Patience Kolb. She has arranged for a sum in the amount of fifty-thousand dollars to be deposited in your name in the First National Bank of Denver. I am sure you have questions that I'll be unable to answer. All she left was this note."

A confused Betty took the letter with shaking hands.

My Dear Betty,

I won't be needing this on my next adventure. I'll be dancing with my beloved Jeffrey. This is to be used for your own adventure.

Love,

Patience Kolb

The man walked away, and Betty turned to Cole. "Who says dreams don't come true?"

Betty leaned over and kissed her husband.

One Year Later

Betty, Diane, and Nan sat on the porch of Bleeker's general store. Cole was inside at the cash register of the store he'd acquired from a retiring Mr. Weatherly.

He and Betty had thought long and hard about what they wanted to do with their newly acquired riches. Unfortunately, the mine was badly damaged in the accident and had to close, so they spent most of the money building a better Bright Valley. When the bank got wind of it, they began investing in the town, and new businesses started popping up. Those businesses were run by the former miners.

Everyone had thought Bright Valley would disappear, but it didn't, thanks to Patience Kolb.

“If I get much bigger, I won’t be able to climb the stairs of our new house," Betty said. "I shouldn't have planned my babies so close together, but it will be fine. Cole is so helpful with Junior."

"The same goes for Jason with little JJ. I'm sure we'll be announcing our second baby soon. Can you believe how we started out? Two strangers on a train. Thank goodness you had the sense to sit next to me," Nan said.

“I have to believe it was meant to be. We had so much in common, and we were both headed for Bright Valley. Now that we endured a winter in Colorado, we can handle anything.”

Cole walked out on the porch. He was always smiling, even more than before. A lifetime in the mine can wear on a man, but he was looking much better. He took Junior from Betty to give her a break. “Are you ladies talking about what wonderful husbands you found in Bright Valley?” he asked jokingly.

“Yes. I married you less than an hour after meeting you, and it was the best thing I ever did,” Betty gushed.

“What about having this little guy?” Cole kissed his son, who cooed.

“Oh, that too. I’ve had so many wonderful things happen here that I can’t pick a best,” Betty said.

"I hope we have many more to come. Betty, you make all my dreams come true. I love you, Mrs. Bleeker."

"I love you too, Mr. Bleeker."

The End

FREE GIFT

Just to say thanks for checking our works we like to gift you

Our Exclusive Never Before Released Books

100% FREE!

Please GO TO

http://cleanromancepublishing.com/gift

And get your FREE gift

Thanks for being such a wonderful client.

Please Check out My Other Works

By checking out the link below

http://cleanromancepublishing.com/fjauth

Thank You

Many thanks for taking the time to buy and read through this book.

It means lots to be supported by SPECIAL readers like YOU.

Hope you enjoyed the book; please support my writing by leaving an honest review to assist other readers.

.

With Regards,

Faith Johnson

Printed in Great Britain
by Amazon